The Costume Ball

Published by Pleasant Company Publications
First published in Great Britain by Penguin Books Ltd., 2002
© 2003 Helen Craig Limited and Katharine Holabird
Based on the text by Katharine Holabird and the illustrations by Helen Craig
From the script by Barbara Slade

The Angelina Ballerina name and character and the dancing Angelina logo are trademarks of
HIT Entertainment PLC, Katharine Holabird, and Helen Craig. ANGELINA is registered
in the U.K. and Japan. The dancing Angelina logo is registered in the U.K.

Visit our Web site at www.americangirl.com and
Angelina's very own site at www.angelinaballerina.com

Printed in the U.S.A.

02 03 04 05 06 07 08 NGS 10 9 8 7 6 5 4 3 2 1

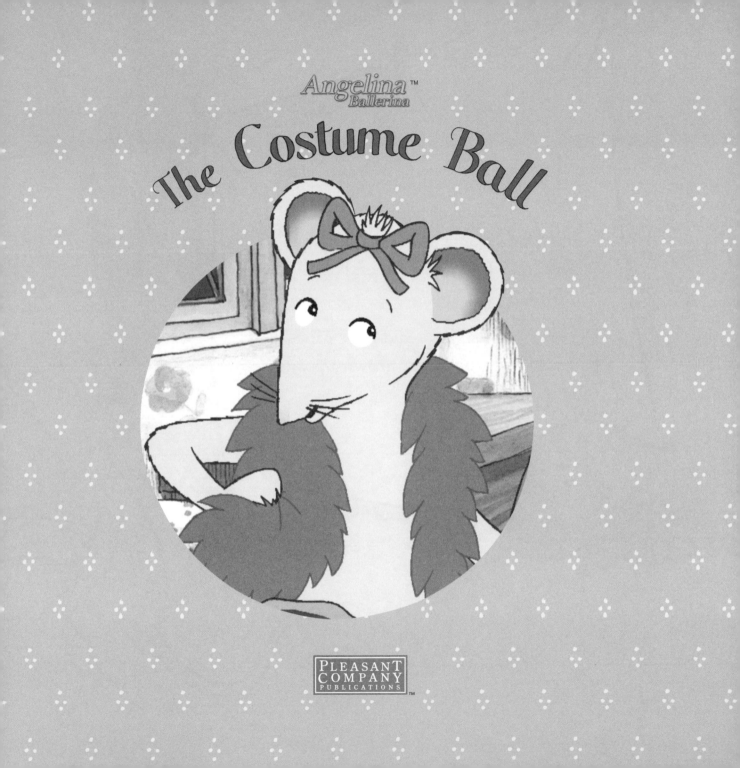

Angelina™
Ballerina

The Costume Ball

PLEASANT
COMPANY
PUBLICATIONS™

It was the day of the costume ball, and Angelina hadn't been invited. "If you're going as a queen and Dad's going as a king, it makes sense that I go as a princess!" she said to Mrs. Mouseling.

"I'm sorry, Angelina," said Mrs. Mouseling patiently. "The ball is for grown-ups, not little mouselings!"

"Everyone should be allowed to go to the ball," complained Angelina to Alice later. Her friend emerged from the dress-up box wearing a hat and a dress that were far too big for her.

Alice danced until she tripped over the hem and fell on top of Angelina. "Sorry!" she giggled. "You could fit us both in this dress!"

"Yes . . ." said Angelina thoughtfully.

It was almost time for the costume ball to begin, and Mrs. Mouseling looked beautiful. "Mrs. Hodgepodge will be here any minute to baby-sit," she said.

"Oh, no!" groaned Angelina. "Last time she kept me awake all night with her horrible snoring!"

"I hope she doesn't bring her cabbage jelly," whispered Alice.

Mr. Mouseling came into the room dressed like a giant bee instead of a king.

"Mix-up at the costume shop!" he explained, as Angelina and Alice giggled.

Just then Mrs. Hodgepodge arrived. "Good night, you two," said Mrs. Mouseling as she swept out the door on Mr. Mouseling's arm. "Be good for Mrs. Hodgepodge!"

After a horrible dinner of cabbage jelly, Angelina and Alice ran upstairs. "I wish we were at the ball," sighed Angelina. "Would you care to dance?"

"I'd love to," said Alice with a smile.

Downstairs, Mrs. Hodgepodge had fallen asleep and was beginning to snore loudly. Angelina was trying to listen to the beautiful music drifting through the window from the ball.

"Come on, Alice!" exclaimed Angelina, as she began rummaging through the dress-up box.

"Come on where?" asked Alice.

"To the costume ball, of course!"

"But what about Mrs. Hodgepodge?" whispered Alice.

"She'll be asleep for hours!" replied Angelina, tossing a hat over to Alice.

As Angelina and Alice entered the hall, they gasped.

"Wow! Look, Alice! It's wonderful!" exclaimed Angelina.
From within their disguise, the two mouselings looked around
them. Angelina wobbled on Alice's shoulders as they tottered
toward a table piled with delicious things to eat.

"All that fooood!" cried Alice.

"Careful, Alice!" whispered Angelina as Alice grabbed a cheese ball.

"Such a wonderful party, don't you agree, my dear?" asked a familiar voice.

It was Miss Lilly!

"Er, yes, Miss . . . miss . . . absolutely unmissable!" stuttered Angelina in her most grown-up voice.

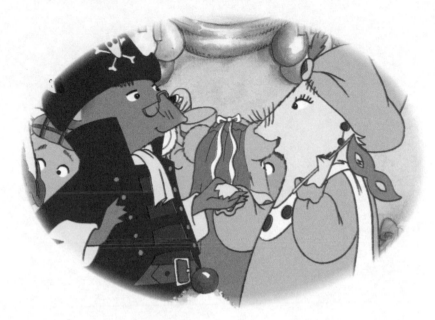

Luckily, just then Dr. Tuttle appeared.

"I was wondering if you'd care to dance?" he asked Miss Lilly.

"It would be a pleasure, darlink!" she replied as she took his paw. "See you later for the Whiskers Reel!" said Miss Lilly to the mouselings as she disappeared.

"I wish someone would ask me to dance," said Angelina glumly as she watched them make their way onto the crowded dance floor.

Back at the Mouseling's cottage, Mrs. Hodgepodge woke up when she felt a draft. "It's coming from Angelina's room," she muttered as she went to investigate. The window was wide open.

At the ball, Angelina was desperate to dance when a voice announced, "Take your positions for the Whiskers Reel!"

"Come on, Alice!" Angelina whispered. Everyone lined up, and the music started.

As they danced, Angelina began to lose her balance on Alice's shoulders. She wobbled and bumped into her father, but luckily he didn't recognize her. Alice and Angelina stumbled into the table, and cheese balls flew everywhere as the two mouselings landed in a big, sticky heap.

Just at that moment, Mrs. Hodgepodge threw open the doors of the hall.

"There they are, those naughty little runaways!" she cried.

"Angelina!" gasped Mr. and Mrs. Mouseling.

Everyone stared at the two mouselings as they sat on the floor, surrounded by cheese balls and trying hard not to cry.

Now they were in real trouble.

Angelina and Alice were up early the next morning. There was a great deal of mess to be cleaned up in the hall.

"My back's aching! This is such hard work!" groaned Alice, mopping the floor.

"I'm so tired! Perhaps going to the ball wasn't such a good idea," sighed Angelina as she scrubbed away.

The door opened, and Mrs. Mouseling came in with
Mrs. Hodgepodge. "We've brought you something
to eat!" said Angelina's mother, smiling.

Angelina and Alice took huge bites from the delicious-
looking sandwiches.

"Oh, no!" they groaned. "Cabbage jelly!"